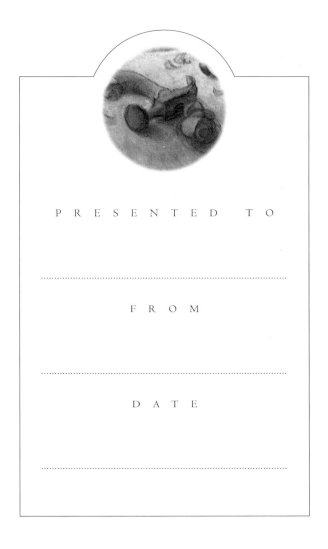

PRESENTED TO

....

FROM

....

DATE

....

You Are Special

ILLUSTRATIONS BY SERGIO MARTINEZ

MAX LUCADO

CROSSWAY BOOKS · WHEATON, ILLINOIS

A DIVISION OF GOOD NEWS PUBLISHERS

PUBLISHER'S ACKNOWLEDGMENT

The publisher wishes to acknowledge that the text for *You Are Special* appeared originally in *Tell Me the Secrets,* written by Max Lucado and illustrated by Ron DiCianni. Special thanks to Ron DiCianni for the idea and vision behind the creation of the series. For more stories in the "Tell Me" series, *Tell Me the Story, Tell Me the Secrets,* and *Tell Me the Promises,* all published by Crossway Books, are available at your local bookstore.

You Are Special
Copyright ©1997 by Max Lucado
Published by Crossway Books
a division of Good News Publishers
1300 Crescent Street
Wheaton, Illinois 60187

Text copyright @ 1997 Max Lucado
Illustrations copyright @ 1997 Sergio Martinez
Design by D² DesignWorks
First printing 1997
Printed in the United States of America
ISBN 0-89107-931-9

LIBRARY OF CONGRESS CATALOGING-IN-PUBLICATION DATA

Lucado, Max.
You are special / Max Lucado.
p. cm.
Summary: Punchinello's opinion of himself changes after talking to his creator.
ISBN 0-89107-931-9 (hc : alk. paper)
[1. Self-esteem--Fiction. 2. Toys--Fiction. 3. Christian life--Fiction. 4. Parables.]
1. Title.   PZ7.L9684   Yo 1997
[E]--dc21   97-5387
                                           CIP
                                           AC

09   08   07   06   05   04   03   02   01   00

26   25   24   23   22   21   20   19   18   17   16   15   14

To the Children
and Children's Ministry
of the Oak Hills Church of Christ

THE WEMMICKS were small
wooden people. All of the wooden
people were carved by a woodworker
named Eli. His workshop sat on a hill
overlooking their village.

Each Wemmick was different.
Some had big noses, others had large eyes.
Some were tall and others were short.
Some wore hats, others wore coats.
But all were made by the same carver and
all lived in the village.

And all day, every day,
the Wemmicks did the same thing:
They gave each other stickers.
Each Wemmick had a box of golden star stickers
and a box of gray dot stickers.
Up and down the streets all over the city,
people spent their days sticking stars
or dots on one another.

The pretty ones,
those with smooth wood and fine paint,
always got stars.
But if the wood was rough or the paint chipped,
the Wemmicks gave dots.

The talented ones got stars, too.
Some could lift big sticks high above
their heads or jump over tall boxes.
Still others knew big words
or could sing pretty songs.
Everyone gave them stars.

Some Wemmicks had
stars all over them! Every time they got a
star it made them feel so good!
It made them want to do something else
and get another star.

Others, though, could do little.
They got dots.

Punchinello was one of these.
He tried to jump high like the others, but he always fell.
And when he fell, the others would gather around
and give him dots.

Sometimes when he fell, his wood got scratched,
so the people would give him more dots.

Then when he would try to explain why he fell,
he would say something silly,
and the Wemmicks would give him more dots.

After a while he had so many dots that he didn't
want to go outside. He was afraid he would do something
dumb such as forget his hat or step in the water,
and then people would give him another dot. In fact,
he had so many gray dots that some people would come up
and give him one for no reason at all.

"He deserves lots of dots,"
the wooden people would agree
with one another.
"He's not a good wooden person."

After a while Punchinello believed them.
"I'm not a good Wemmick," he would say.

The few times he went outside,
he hung around other Wemmicks
who had a lot of dots.
He felt better around them.

One day he met a
Wemmick who was unlike any he'd ever met.
She had no dots or stars. She was just wooden.
Her name was Lucia.

It wasn't that people didn't try to give her stickers;
it's just that the stickers didn't stick.
Some of the Wemmicks admired Lucia for having no dots,
so they would run up and give her a star.
But it would fall off.
Others would look down on her for having no stars,
so they would give her a dot.
But it wouldn't stay either.

That's the way I want to be, thought Punchinello.
I don't want anyone's marks.
So he asked the stickerless Wemmick how she did it.

"It's easy," Lucia replied. "Every day I go see Eli."

"Eli?"

"Yes, Eli. The woodcarver. I sit in the workshop with him."

"Why?"

"Why don't you find out for yourself?
Go up the hill. He's there."
And with that the Wemmick who had no stickers
turned and skipped away.

"But will he want to see me?"
Punchinello cried out.
Lucia didn't hear.
So Punchinello went home.
He sat near a window
and watched the wooden people
as they scurried around
giving each other stars and dots.
"It's not right,"
he muttered to himself.
And he decided to go see Eli.

He walked up the narrow path to the top of the hill
and stepped into the big shop. His wooden eyes widened at the
size of everything. The stool was as tall as he was.
He had to stretch on his tiptoes to see the top of the workbench.
A hammer was as long as his arm. Punchinello swallowed hard.
"I'm not staying here!" and he turned to leave.

Then he heard his name.

"Punchinello?" The voice was deep and strong.

Punchinello stopped.

"Punchinello! How good to see you.
Come and let me have a look at you."

Punchinello turned slowly and looked at the large bearded craftsman.
"You know my name?" the little Wemmick asked.

"Of course I do. I made you."

Eli stooped down and picked him up
and set him on the bench. "Hmm," the maker spoke thoughtfully
as he looked at the gray dots.
"Looks like you've been given some bad marks."

"I didn't mean to, Eli. I really tried hard."

"Oh, you don't have to defend yourself to me, child.
I don't care what the other Wemmicks think."

"You don't?"

"No, and you shouldn't either. Who are they to give stars or dots?
They're Wemmicks just like you.
What they think doesn't matter, Punchinello.
All that matters is what I think.
And I think you are pretty special."

Punchinello laughed.
"Me, special? Why?
I can't walk fast. I can't jump.
My paint is peeling.
Why do I matter to you?"

Eli looked at Punchinello,
put his hands on those small wooden
shoulders, and spoke very slowly.
"Because you're mine.
That's why you matter to me."

Punchinello had never
had anyone look at him like this—
much less his maker.
He didn't know what to say.

27

"Every day I've been hoping you'd come," Eli explained.

"I came because I met someone who had no marks,"
said Punchinello.

"I know. She told me about you."

"Why don't the stickers stay on her?"

The maker spoke softly.
"Because she has decided that what I think is more important than
what they think. The stickers only stick if you let them."

"What?"

"The stickers only stick if they matter to you.
The more you trust my love,
the less you care about their stickers."

"I'm not sure I understand."